A NOTE TO PARENTS

When your children are ready to "step into reading," giving them the right books is as crucial as giving them the right food to eat. **Step into Reading Books** present exciting stories and information reinforced with lively, colorful illustrations that make learning to read fun, satisfying, and worthwhile. They are priced so that acquiring an entire library of them is affordable. And they are beginning readers with a difference—they're written on five levels.

Early Step into Reading Books are designed for brand-new readers, with large type and only one or two lines of very simple text per page. **Step 1 Books** feature the same easy-to-read type as the Early Step into Reading Books, but with more words per page. **Step 2 Books** are both longer and slightly more difficult, while **Step 3 Books** introduce readers to paragraphs and fully developed plot lines. **Step 4 Books** offer exciting nonfiction for the increasingly independent reader.

The grade levels assigned to the five steps—preschool through kindergarten for the Early Books, preschool through grade 1 for Step 1, grades 1 through 3 for Step 2, grades 2 through 3 for Step 3, and grades 2 through 4 for Step 4—are intended only as guides. Some children move through all five steps very rapidly; others climb the steps over a period of several years. Either way, these books will help your child "step into reading" in style!

For Mom and Dad, once again.
From your best home run ever!

—K. C.

Text copyright © 2000 by Kathryn Cristaldi McKeon.
Illustrations copyright © 2000 by Abby Carter.
All rights reserved under International and Pan-American Copyright Conventions.
Published in the United States by Random House, Inc., New York, and simultaneously
in Canada by Random House of Canada Limited, Toronto.

www.randomhouse.com/kids

Library of Congress Cataloging-in-Publication Data
McKeon, Kathryn Cristaldi.
Baseball ballerina strikes out / by Kathryn Cristaldi McKeon ; illustrated by Abby Carter.
p.   cm. — (Step into reading. A step 2 book)
SUMMARY: With the help of her coach, a young girl teaches two bullies a lesson and
leads her team to victory in the play-offs.
ISBN 0-679-89132-3 (pbk.) — ISBN 0-679-99132-8 (lib. bdg.)
[1. Baseball—Fiction. 2. Bullies—Fiction.]
I. Carter, Abby, ill. II. Title. III. Series: Step into reading.
Step 2 book. PZ7.M4786763Bas 2000 [Fic]—dc21 98-32040

Printed in the United States of America April 2000 10 9 8 7 6 5 4 3 2 1

STEP INTO READING, RANDOM HOUSE, and the Random House colophon are registered
trademarks and the Step into Reading colophon is a trademark of Random House, Inc.

Step into Reading®

Baseball Ballerina Strikes Out!

A Step 2 Book

by Kathryn Cristaldi
illustrated by Abby Carter

Random House 🏠 New York

I love baseball.

I am on a team called the Sharks.

My coach calls me a

baseball ballerina.

That is because I play baseball.

And I take ballet lessons.

At first I did not like ballet.

But it is not so bad.

We do neat spins and twirls.

Madame says I am

the fastest spinner

in my class.

I tell her that I practice spinning

at home—

in the clothes dryer!

Then I laugh.

Madame does not.

She never laughs at my jokes.

Mr. Lee is my baseball coach.

He is very different from Madame.

He likes to tell jokes

and play pranks.

Once he came to practice

dressed in a gorilla suit.

He growled at us

if we missed a play.

Then he handed out bananas
at the end of practice.

Mr. Lee says that ballet has
helped my game.
"In ballet you have to keep
on your toes," he tells me.
"The same goes for baseball."

Good thing I do not have to wear
a tutu on the baseball field!

One day at practice

Mr. Lee says,

"Listen up!

Next week are the play-offs.

We will play against the Beavers."

He hands out new Sharks hats.

My team cheers.

I stick out my two front teeth.

"Oh, no," I say,

pretending to be a beaver.

"We are going to be eaten—

<u>by sharks</u>!"

Everyone cracks up—even Mr. Lee.

I walk home

with my friend Mary Ann.

We turn left onto Cedar.

We make a right on Willow.

Suddenly two boys ride up

on bikes.

They are the Colby twins,

Cal and Kyle.

CEDAR

Cal grabs my new Sharks hat.

He throws the hat to Kyle.

"Give it back," I try to say,

but my voice comes out

in a squeak.

"Squeak!" says Cal.

"Mousey wants her hat back,"

says Kyle.

He throws my hat

into a puddle.

The Colby twins race off.

"Stupid bullies!" Mary Ann screams.

On Thursday we play against
the Beavers.

I steal a base.

I catch two pop flies.

And I hit <u>four</u> home runs!

"You are turning into
my star player," says Mr. Lee.

The next day

Mary Ann and I

walk to school together.

We are at the playground

when I hear it.

"Squeak!"

I know who it is.

It is the Colby twins.

"Hey, Mousey," says Kyle.

"Got any cheese?"

Cal grabs my lunchbox.

He dumps it into a garbage can.

"Stupid bullies!"

Mary Ann screams.

I open my mouth,

but no words come out.

My heart goes

<u>thump</u>, <u>thump</u>, <u>thump</u>.

Our last play-off game is

after school.

We are playing against

the Tigers.

"We're gr-r-r-eat!"

shout the Tigers.

My team scores two runs.

Now it is my turn at bat.

"Here comes my star player,"

says Mr. Lee.

I step up to the plate.

"Home run! Home run!"

scream the Sharks.

Then I hear it.

"Squeak!

Hey, look! Mousey plays ball!"

It is the Colby twins.

My knees start to shake.

My heart goes

<u>thump</u>, <u>thump</u>, <u>thump</u>.

The pitcher throws the ball.

I swing and I miss.

Strike one!

Strike two!

Strike three!

I am out.

I walk back to the dugout.

"You will do better next time,"

says Mr. Lee.

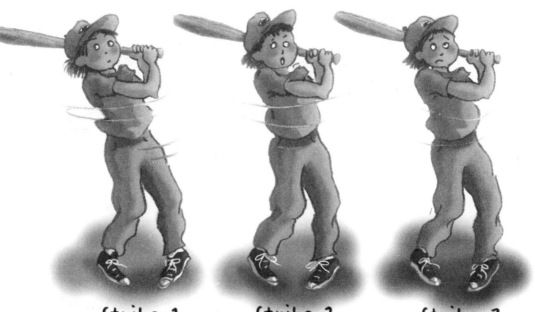

Strike 1 Strike 2 Strike 3

Out

But I do not do better.

I strike out four more times.

The Sharks still win the game.

Now we will be in the championships.

Everyone is excited.

Except me.

"I have to do something
about the Colby twins,"
I tell Mary Ann.
"They are ruining my game."

Mary Ann's mom is waiting
in the bleachers.
"How about a snack?" she says.
She hands us each a banana.

I pretend I am a monkey.

"Ooo! Ooo! Eee! Eee!" I screech.

Mary Ann giggles.

"You make a great monkey,"
she says.

Just then I get an idea.

I run to the dugout

to talk to Mr. Lee.

I tell him about

the bully problem.

Then I tell him about my plan.

He listens.

Then he laughs.

"Okay," says my coach.

"Anything for my star player."

He gives me a wink.

The next day after practice,

I tell Mary Ann my plan.

We walk home together.

We make a left on Cedar.

We make a right on Willow.

Two kids on bikes race up to us.

"Hey, Mousey!" they shout.

It is the Colby twins.

Cal grabs my Sharks hat.

He throws it to Kyle.

Just then there is a noise.

"Roar!"

A gorilla jumps out of the bushes.

Kyle drops my hat.

The gorilla picks up Cal
with one arm.
He picks up Kyle
with the other.

"Help!" squeaks Cal.

"Help!" squeaks Kyle.

"Don't worry," I say.

"It is only Oscar.

He must have escaped

from the zoo."

I stare into the gorilla's eyes.

"Ooo! Ooo! Eee! Eee!" I shout.

"Eee! Eee! Ooo! Ooo!"

the gorilla answers.

Then he drops the Colby twins.

"W-w-wow!" says Cal.

"C-c-cool!" says Kyle.

They race off down the block.

"You did it!" Mary Ann shouts.

"You really got them good."

We give each other high fives.

I shake the gorilla's hand.

"Thanks," I say.

"No problem,"

says the gorilla.

On Tuesday it is

the championship game.

We are playing the Rattlesnakes.

"Hiss! Hiss!" they call

from the field.

It is my turn at bat.

"Home run! Home run!"

scream the Sharks.

Then I hear another sound.

"Ooo! Ooo! Eee! Eee!"

It is the Colby twins.

They smile and wave to me

from the stands.

The pitcher throws.

SMACK!

It is a home run!

I hit five home runs

before the game is over.

We win the championship!

"My star player is back,"

says Mr. Lee.

He gives me a wink.

"Bananas for everyone!"

he says.